Giants'
Castle

Shribble
Gorge

ETTINSMOOR

Lally's Rock

THE GIANT SURPRISE

A Narnia Story

by Hiawyn Oram

illustrated by Tudor Humphries

HARPERCOLLINSPUBLISHERS

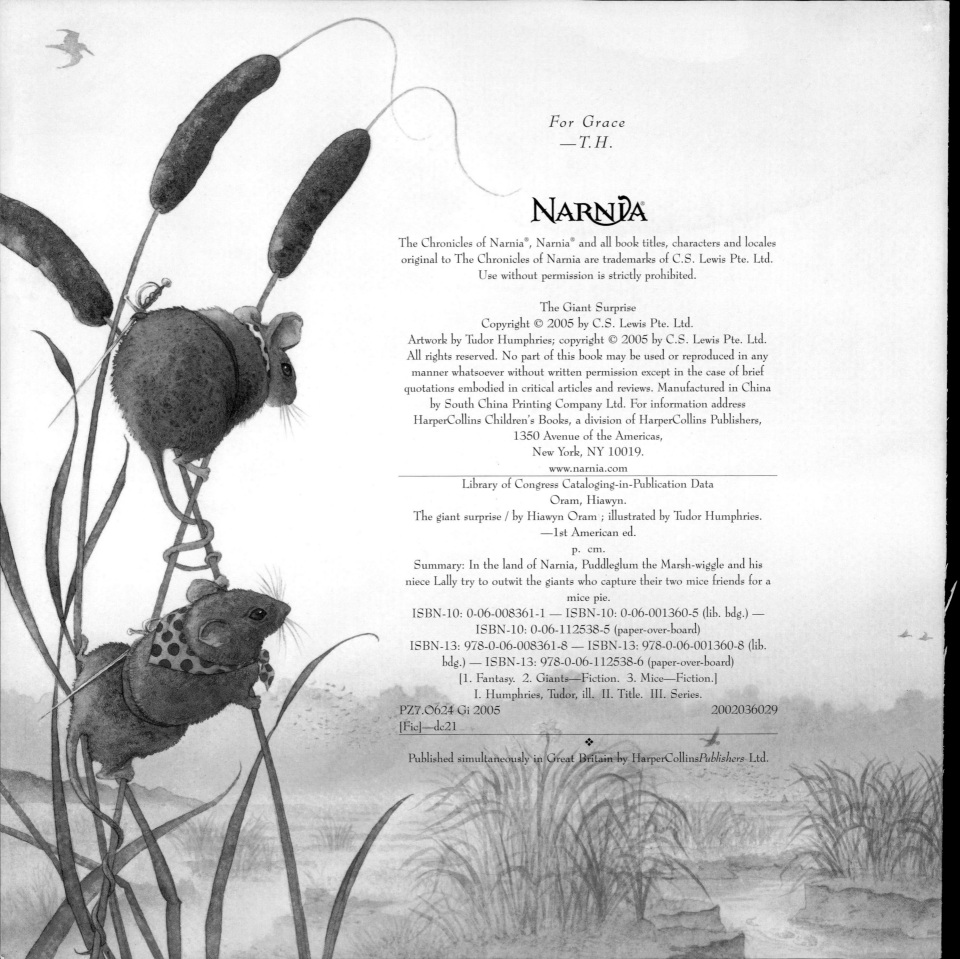

For Grace
—T.H.

NARNIA®

The Giant Surprise
Copyright © 2005 by C.S. Lewis Pte. Ltd.
Artwork by Tudor Humphries; copyright © 2005 by C.S. Lewis Pte. Ltd.
All rights reserved. No part of this book may be used or reproduced in any
manner whatsoever without written permission except in the case of brief
quotations embodied in critical articles and reviews. Manufactured in China
by South China Printing Company Ltd. For information address
HarperCollins Children's Books, a division of HarperCollins Publishers,
1350 Avenue of the Americas,
New York, NY 10019.
www.narnia.com

Library of Congress Cataloging-in-Publication Data
Oram, Hiawyn.
The giant surprise / by Hiawyn Oram ; illustrated by Tudor Humphries.
—1st American ed.
p. cm.
Summary: In the land of Narnia, Puddleglum the Marsh-wiggle and his
niece Lally try to outwit the giants who capture their two mice friends for a
mice pie.
ISBN-10: 0-06-008361-1 — ISBN-10: 0-06-001360-5 (lib. bdg.) —
ISBN-10: 0-06-112538-5 (paper-over-board)
ISBN-13: 978-0-06-008361-8 — ISBN-13: 978-0-06-001360-8 (lib.
bdg.) — ISBN-13: 978-0-06-112538-6 (paper-over-board)
[1. Fantasy. 2. Giants—Fiction. 3. Mice—Fiction.]
I. Humphries, Tudor, ill. II. Title. III. Series.
PZ7.O624 Gi 2005   2002036029
[Fic]—dc21

❖

Published simultaneously in Great Britain by HarperCollins*Publishers* Ltd.

Narnia . . .
A world made of magic from the start of time . . .
full of marvelous creatures, talking beasts
and trees that sometimes get up and dance.
Now pull on your boots . . .
and splash through the muddy marshlands,
home to the web-footed, web-fingered Marsh-
wiggles. Meet Puddleglum, the most famous of
them all. Get to know his niece, Lally, the brave
little Wigglet, as together they help the marsh mice
challenge the roaring, rock-throwing, not-so-clever
giants of Shribble Gorge!

It all started one otherwise peaceful morning . . .

Puddleglum was fishing and Lally was playing with her boat when two marsh mice pushed through the reeds.

"There's a terrible roaring going on!" said Greep.

"And sloshing and galoshing," added Graypaw from behind.

Puddleglum sniffed the air. "Giants," he said gloomily.

"But it can't be!" said Lally. "Giants never come to our marshes!"

"Believe me," said Puddleglum. "These giants do. And they're not just getting closer. They're *here*!"

"*Stand and fight!*" cried Greep.

"*Fight and stand!*" cried Graypaw.

"*Dive and swim!*" cried Puddleglum.

Lally dived. Puddleglum dived after her as up roared

the Giant Dribble and the Giant Crackerwhack,

waving giant fishing rods.

In a flash, one hooked Greep

and the other hooked Graypaw.

"Let us down!" squealed
Greep. "You great big
mice-catching giants!"
"Let us down this very
minute or be sorry!!"
squeaked Graypaw.
But the giants
took no notice.

Dangling Greep and Graypaw in the air, they turned on their heels
and strode off the way they'd come . . . GALLYSHLOOP . . . GALLYSHLOP!

"After them!" cried Lally.

"Yes, after us!" cried the mice. "And hurry!"

Puddleglum put Lally on his shoulders and set off.
His legs were like stilts, his feet like paddles. He knew the land
like the back of his hand, and he was never far behind.

GALLYSHLOOP,

GALLYSHLOP!

But when they arrived at the giants' gorge, there was no sign of
Greep or Graypaw . . . only roaring, raging, not-very-clever
rock-and-rubble-throwing
Giants!

Dodging boots and bits of boulder,
Puddleglum sprang from rock to rock
until he found Dribble and Crackerwhack.

"Where are our mice?" he demanded.

The giants looked blank. Then a big beam
broke across Dribble's face.

**"Aaah . . . mice! Us remember!
Us catch mice. Lots of mice!"**

But when a rock whizzed by,
he forgot what he was saying
and roared off for a game of Rock Shies.

Lally shivered. "Do you think
they've already eaten them?"

"Worse," said Puddleglum. "I think
they're collecting them to make
one big Mice Pie. Now, can
you keep them busy while
I look around?"

Lally's heart sank.
"All right," she sighed.
"I'll try."

Even though she was trembling
and the rock was hard,
Lally managed some of her best cartwheels.
The giants were so surprised
that, one by one,
they gathered around.
When Lally saw she had their full
attention, she took a deep breath
and shouted,
"Listen, giants!
We're going to
play a game!"

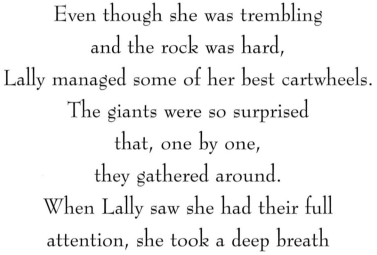

"GAME! GAME!" roared the giants.
"GAME OF ROCK SHIES!"

"No!" Lally yelled back firmly.
"A game of . . ." What?

Her mind raced. What game
could a little Wigglet play with
these giant rock throwers?
Then suddenly she had it . . .
one of her good ideas.

"*A game of . . .
making things!*"

US REMEMBER! US MAKING MICE PIE!"

"No!" yelled Lally. *"Rock sandwiches! Much better!"*

"ROCK SANDWICHES!" roared the giants. **"YUM! YUM! YUM!"**

"Now first, for the filling," said Lally, "we take a lot of rocks and crush them well."

"LOT OF ROCKS!" roared the giants.
"CRUSH 'EM WELL!"
   They rushed around collecting rocks, crushing rocks
with rock hammers, and all the time roaring,

"YUM! YUM! YUM!"

"Very good!" said Lally. "And for the bread . . .
slices of fresh hills!"

"Not too thick, mind," she called after them. "Medium thin!"

And all the time she had the giants slicing,

Puddleglum was looking
for Greep and Graypaw.
High and low he searched—
up the gorge, in every gully—
until he came to the giants'
tumbledown castle.

Here at last he heard what he was beginning to fear he never would—
the sound of mice, lots of mice, coming from the rocked-up larder.
And over their squeaking and squealing and scampering and panicking
was Greep's voice trying to calm them,

"Gally up! Gally ho! Stand your ground!
Never let a giant jelly your legs!"

"Greep! Graypaw! All of you!" Puddleglum called. "Hold on and I'll soon have you out!"

And while he used a giant corkscrew to make holes in the larder and free the mice . . .

Lally sent the giants to the river for lots of gooey mud ketchup.

"YUM! YUM! YUM!" they drooled as they scooped it up and slapped it on.

"ROCK SANDWICHES READY! US EAT!"

They smacked their lips.   They bit in.

Their cheeks bulged.

Their teeth ground.

Lally could hardly believe it.
"*Stop! Stop!*
You don't understand!
This is a game! We don't eat
the sandwiches!"

But there was no stopping
the giants.

"*Oh no!*" Lally cried.
"This has gone too far!
Uncle Puddleglum!

HELP!"

"Right here!" said Puddleglum, leaping up beside her. "And whatever you did, it was just the thing. You kept the giants busy and I found the mice."

"But look!" cried Lally. "They're eating rocks and hills and mud! We have to stop them! They might choke or—"

"Don't worry," said Puddleglum. "Watch this!" He picked up a small rock . . . and another . . . and another . . . and hurled them down on to the plain.

At once the giants forgot about eating.

"ROCK SHIES!" they roared. "US REMEMBER!
US PLAY ROCK SHIES!"
And their rock throwing began all over again,

only this time with pieces of
hilly, muddy, rock sandwiches!

"Poor old giants," said Lally as Puddleglum led them all safely home. "I expect they even throw rocks in their sleep!"

"If they remember to sleep!" said Graypaw.

"Well, it's lucky they forgot to eat!" said Greep. "Or we'd be Mice Pie."

"And you still could be," said Puddleglum, "so prepare for the worst and it won't catch you by surprise."

"Well, I *much* prefer thinking the best," said Lally when they were settled by the fire. "And that was a big adventure I won't forget in a hurry!"

"True, true," sighed Puddleglum. "Nothing like adventure to remind us life isn't all fishing and mud-winkle stew. So what's next, I wonder. Ogres? Dragons?"

"Whatever it is," said Lally, "when it comes, I know where I want to be."

"So do we," said the mice softly . . .

"With the bravest Marsh-wiggle
and the bravest little Wigglet
in all of Narnia!"

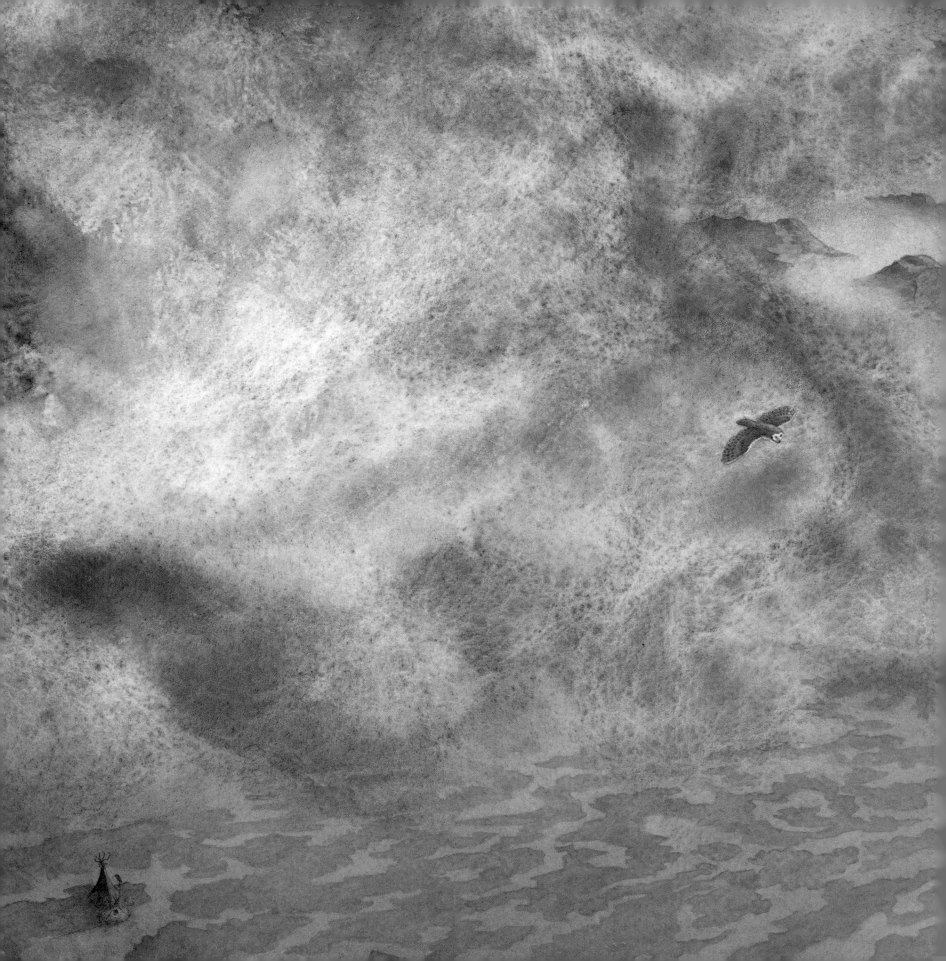